Having Fun

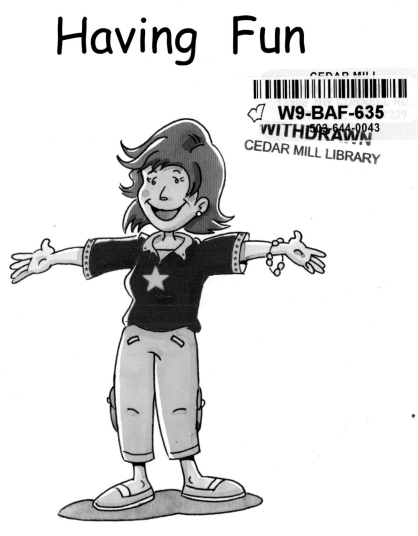

written by Pam Holden
illustrated by Kelvin Hawley

1

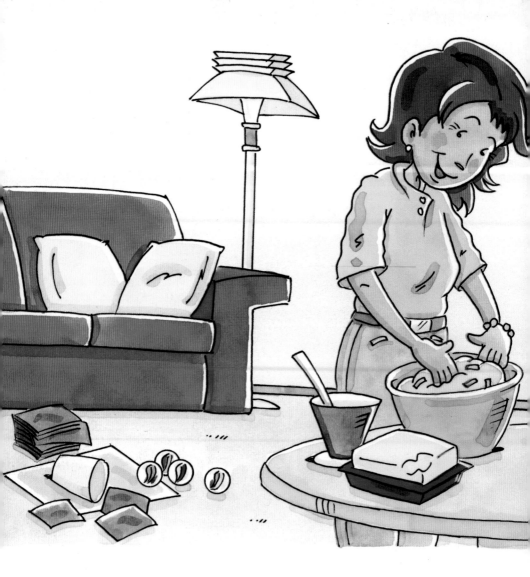

C is for cake.

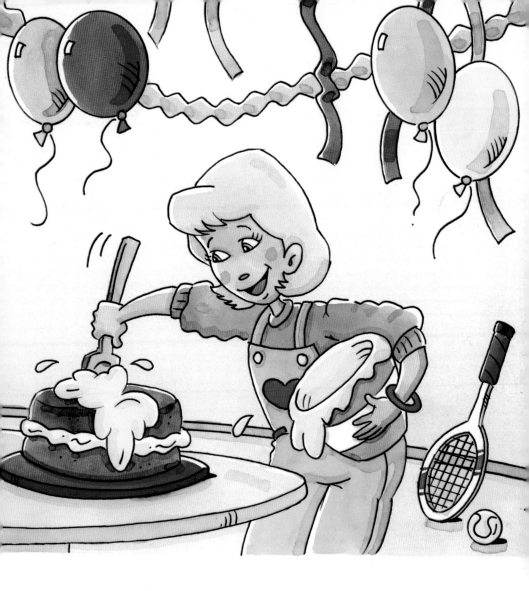

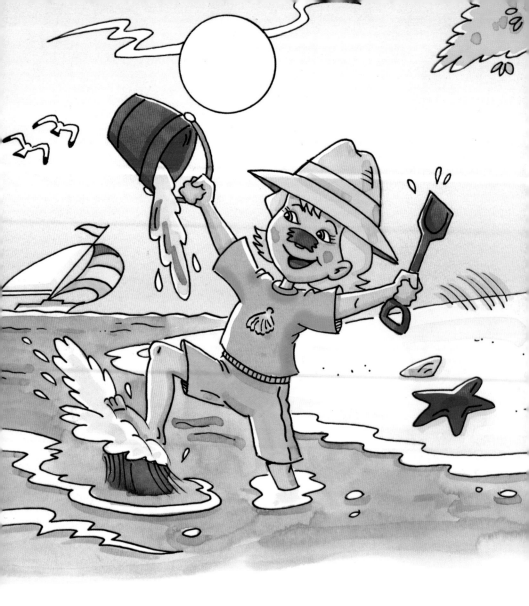

B is for beach.

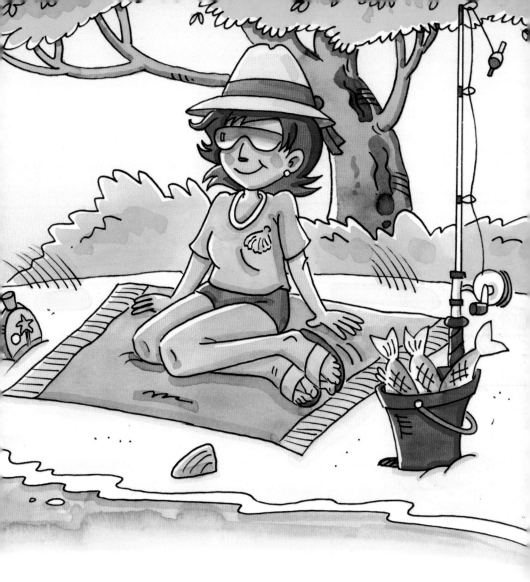

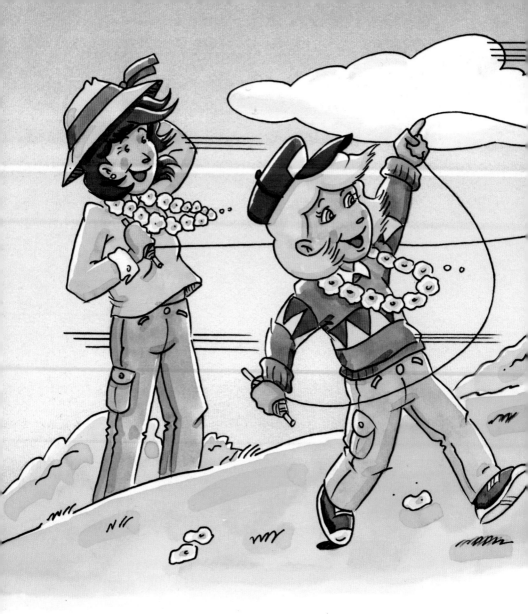

K is for kites.

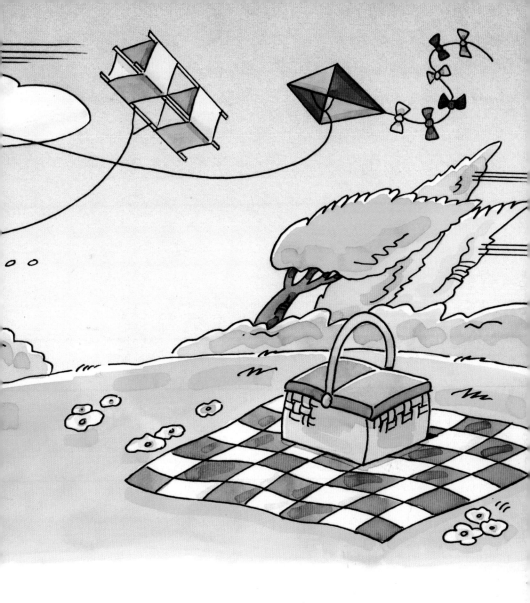

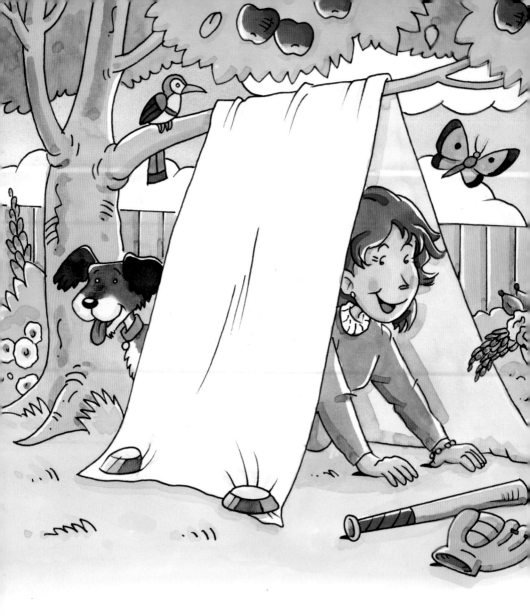

G is for garden.

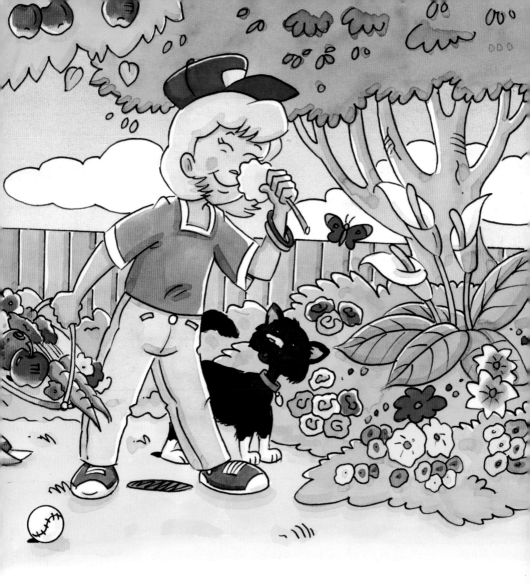

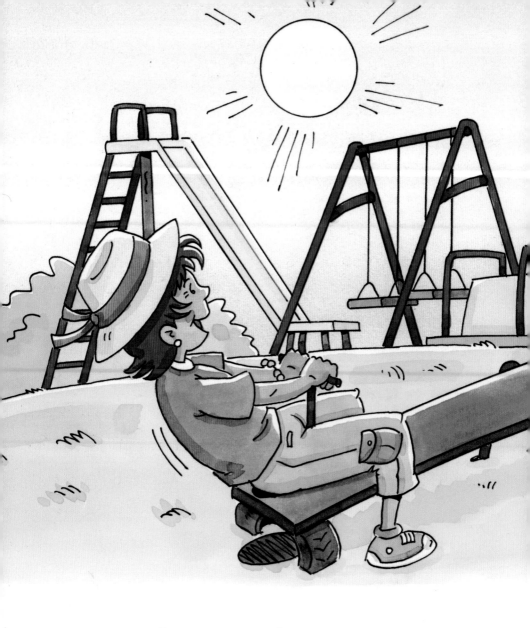

P is for playground.

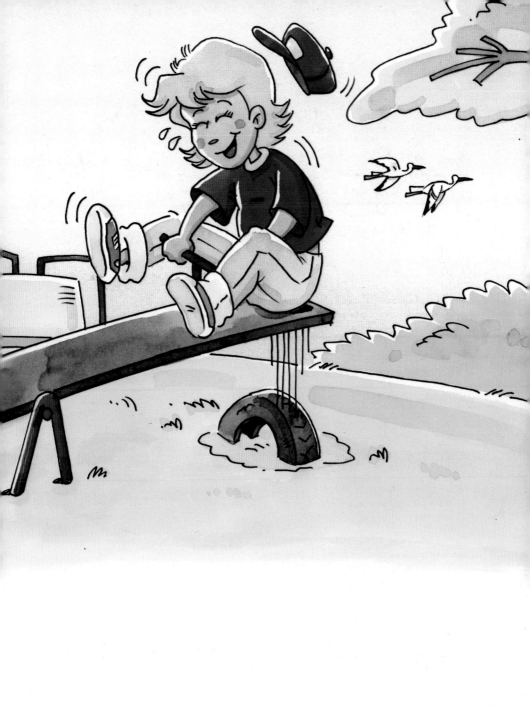

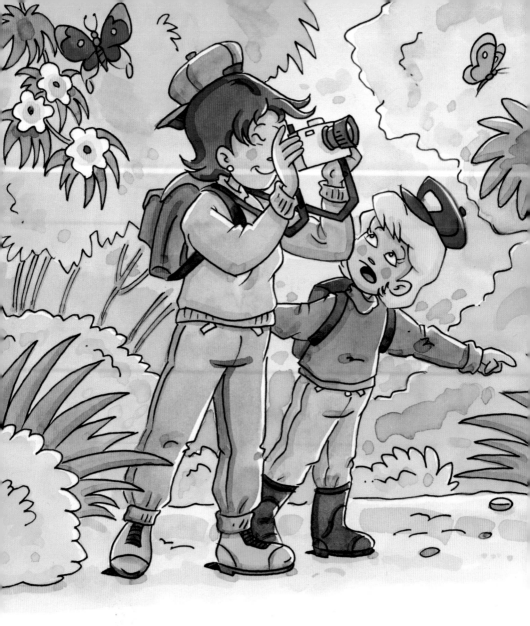

W is for walk.

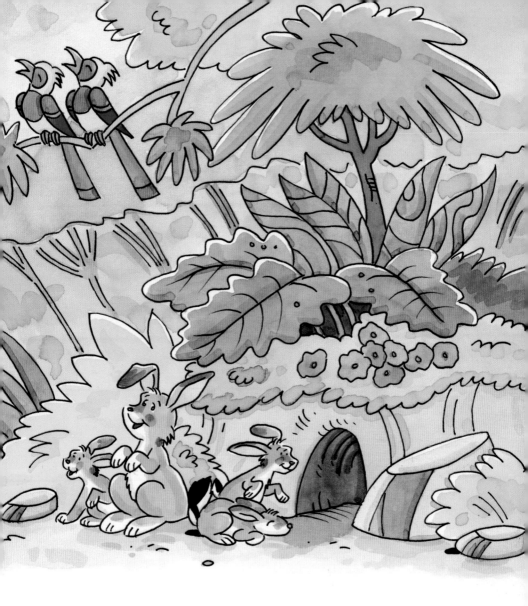

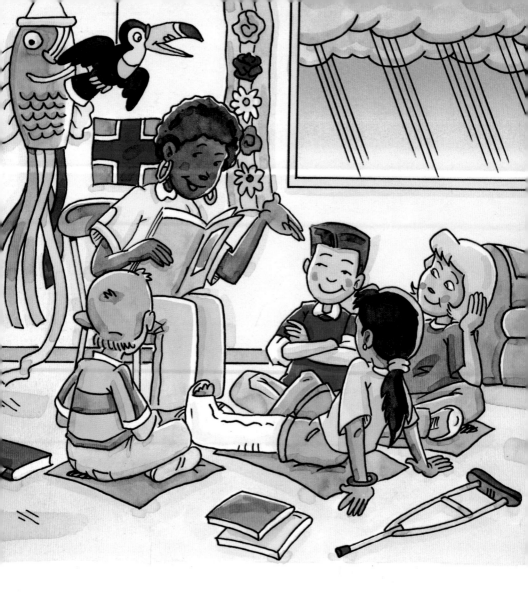

L is for library.

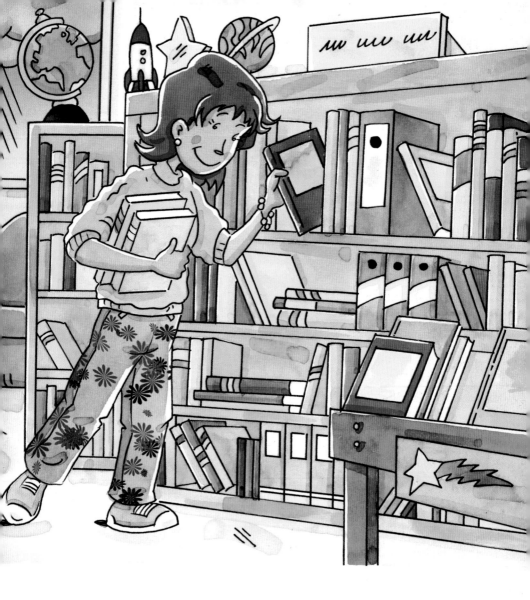

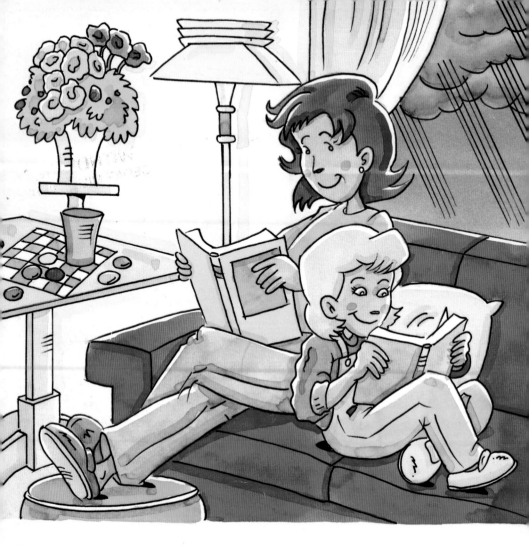

B is for books.